# Tabby McTat

By Julia Donaldson

Illustrated by Axel Scheffler

ALISON
GREEN
BOOKS

Tabby McTat was a busker's cat
With a miaow that was loud and strong.
The two of them sang of this and that,
And people threw coins in the old checked hat,
And this was their favourite song:

*"Me, you and the old guitar,*
*How perfectly, perfectly happy we are.*
*MEEE-EW and the old guitar,*
*How PURRRR-fectly happy we are."*

One morning, while Fred ate some bacon and bread,
McTat took a stroll round the block,

Then stopped – for there on a doorstep sat
A gorgeously glossy and green-eyed cat.
She was black with one snowy white sock.

Sock and McTat had a cat-to-cat chat
And that's how their story began,
For while they were chatting of this and of that . . .

A thief had his eye on the old checked hat.
He eyed it. He snatched it. He ran!

The busker gave chase but he tripped on a lace
And crash! In a flash he was down.

He broke his leg and he banged his head

And he ended up in a hospital bed
In a faraway part of town.

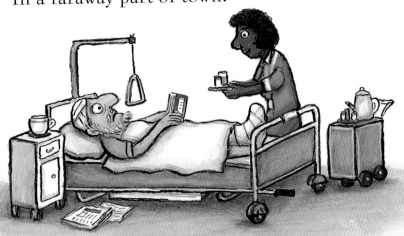

"Goodbye," McTat said. "I must get back to Fred."

But where had the busker gone?

The sun went down and the sky grew black.
The stars came out, but he didn't come back.
McTat lingered on . . . and on.

A week later, Sock took a stroll round the block
And found her new friend looking thin.
"He's gone off and left me!" said Tabby McTat.

Then Sock said, "My people, Prunella and Pat,
Would gladly find room for a fine tabby cat."

She was right, and they took McTat in.

Next morning, old Fred left his hospital bed
And found his way back to the square,
But a brass band stood where the pair once sat
And the band played this and the band played that,
And Fred looked all round for his loud-miaowed cat,
But Tabby McTat wasn't there!

NO
BUSKING

And he pulled out this . . .

and he pulled out that . . .

And people threw coins in the tall black hat,
But the busker was never there.

One morning Sock said, "Look under the bed
And see the three kittens I've had!"

And Soames looked like this,             and Susan like that,

And the littlest kitten, called Samuel Sprat,
Looked exactly the same as his dad.

The three kittens grew and they learnt how to mew,
And McTat sometimes sang them his song.

And Samuel Sprat with his tabby-grey fur
Had a deafening miaow and a very loud purr
And he simply loved singing along:

*"Me, you and the old guitar,*
*How perfectly, perfectly happy we are.*
*MEEE-EW and the old guitar,*
*How PURRRR-fectly happy we are."*

When Susan and Soames found very good homes
Their parents were happy and proud.

There was one home like this . . .

and another like that . . .

But nobody wanted poor Samuel Sprat.
They all said, "His voice is too loud."

Now Tabby McTat was a home-loving cat
But he couldn't stop dreaming of Fred.

And one day he called for his wife and his son
And he told them,
    "There's something that has to be done.
    I *must* go and find him," he said.

So up and down . . .

and all over town . . .

He wandered a whole week long,